Brave
Little Penguin

for Isabella, Cara and Matt, my little penguins
...and for Mark, fearless and fun.
– A.P.

First published in 2008 by Scholastic Australia
This edition first published in 2009 by Scholastic Children's Books
Euston House, 24 Eversholt Street
London NW1 1DB
a division of Scholastic Ltd
www.scholastic.co.uk
London ~ New York ~ Toronto ~ Sydney ~ Auckland
Mexico City ~ New Delhi ~ Hong Kong

ISBN 978 1407 11577 1

10 9 8 7 6 5 4 3 2 1

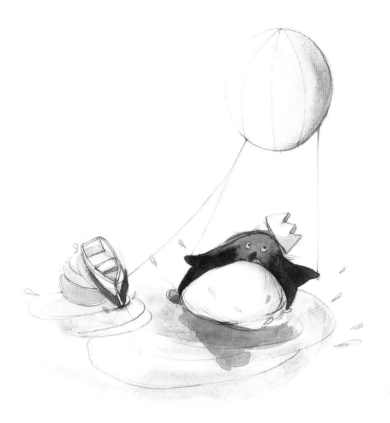

Brave
Little Penguin

SCHOLASTIC

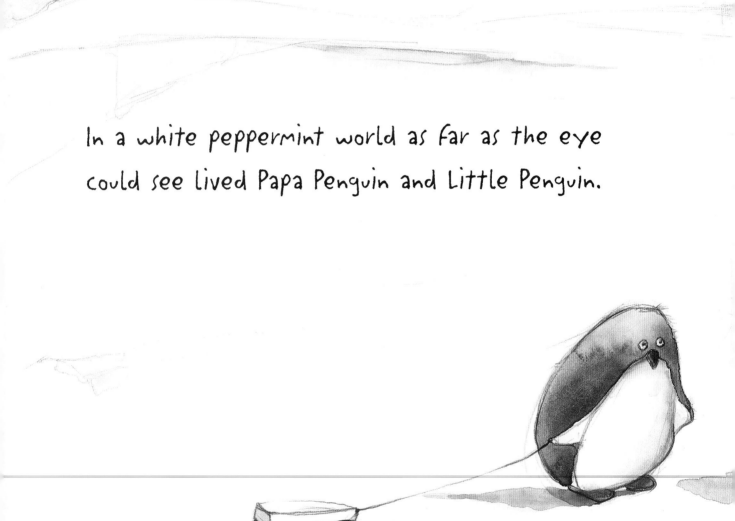

In a white peppermint world as far as the eye could see lived Papa Penguin and Little Penguin.

'Wait here, Little Penguin,
I'll be back soon,' said Papa Penguin.

They snuggled up
close and the winter
weather sighed.

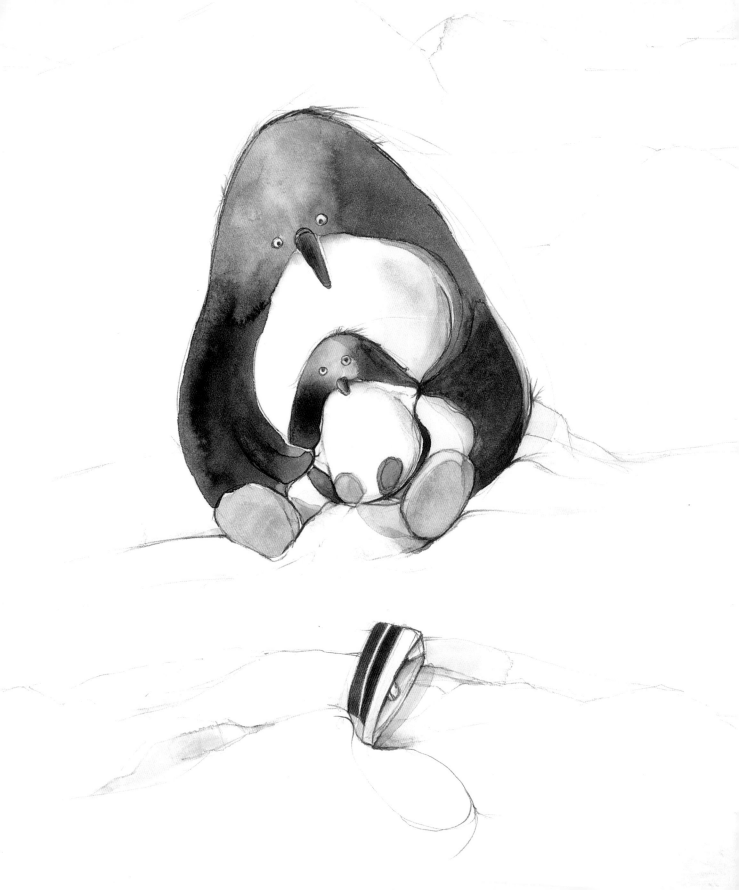

'What will I do?' asked Little Penguin.

'Imagine you are in charge of the icicle mountain. I will be back before the moon,' said Papa Penguin.

'Back before the moon,' called Little Penguin
as Papa Penguin waddled away.

Little Penguin felt sad.

But Little Penguin
decided to be brave.

Little Penguin marched
with icy soldiers

to the top of the icicle mountain . . .

. . . and then

slippery-dipped

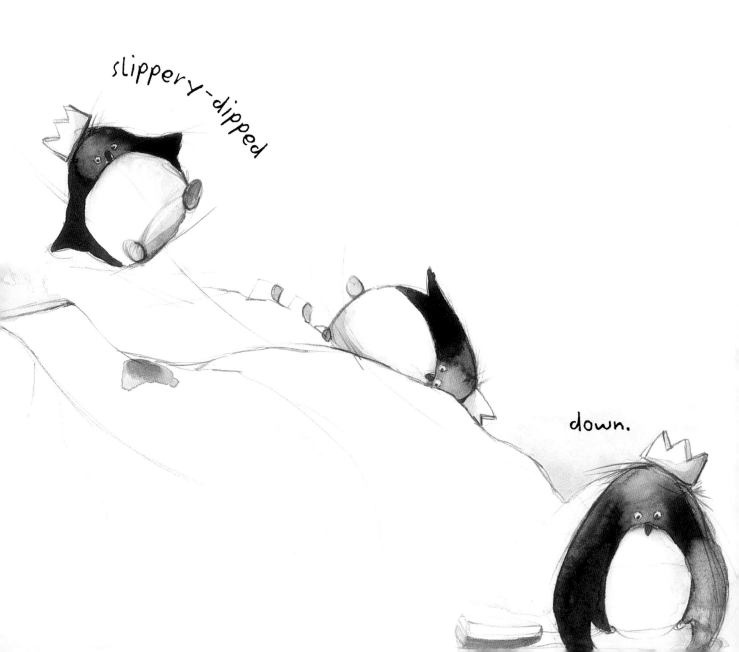

down.

Little Penguin floated over the ice

to a forest of treasure,

and made a fortress to keep home safe.

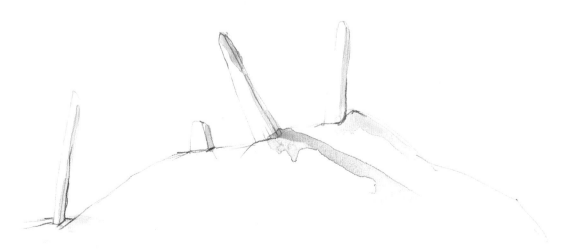

Little Penguin sailed boaty

far and wide

over rolling seas . . .

. . . and back home through a wild, wild storm.

The white peppermint world

turned red and orange and purple.

And just as the big silver moon began
to peep through the clouds . . .

'I'm back,' said Papa Penguin.

And together Papa Penguin and
Little Penguin called
the stars in one by one.